TO TRAIN A FALCON

A FICTIONAL SHORT STORY

Self-Published by
Sarah M. Wasson

ISBN: 979-8-3302-3788-3

Chapter 1

"Father, when will my training start?" Charlie asked his father excitedly. He had often asked him this question but never received an answer. He overheard his parents talking about his future the other night and thought maybe he would get the response he so wanted to hear.

"Um, when you are older," his father replied between cutting leather strips.

"How old must I be?" He said eagerly, probing for more information.

"When you turn fourteen, my son. You will be allowed to attend Selection Day, and you can pick Falconry." Charlie beamed up at him, his brown eyes lit up. Less than a year to wait, but then his face slowly slid into a frown.

"I thought I could skip Selection Day and just follow in your footsteps." His father shook his head. "Well, after I chose Falconry, what will my first duties be as an apprentice?" He asked, barely being able to contain himself.

"If you are chosen to be an apprentice, you will clean and repair the equipment with several other boys your age," he said proudly.

"Equipment? That's all?" Charlie said in disappointment. He did not hear his father say the word *if*.

His father placed the leather jess that he was working on down. "All apprentices start with the equipment. After you have mastered that duty, you and the other apprentices will be in charge of feeding the dogs. You will learn all you need to learn after Selection Day. I must be off." His father patted him on the shoulder and departed the house.

Charlie sat at the table with his arms crossed. "Cleaning the equipment, really, that's it," he grumbled, racking his hands through his messy brown hair.

Charlie's father, Kenton, was the Master Falconer for King Robert the Loved. The Master Falconer was a very prestigious position in the King's Court. Charlie had hoped that being the Master Falconer's son, he would be able to advance to bird handling straight off. He had been around the birds before he could even talk.

Each year, his father selected a few boys to become apprentices. Each apprentice would be teamed with a Court Falconer to train under, and someday they would become falconers themselves. Every Lord and governor in the Kingdom had one or more falconers in their court, and they all wanted at least one trained by the King's Master Falconer himself.

In the Kingdon of Weshingham, the number of birds a noble had was a show of their wealth and standing in the court.

Charlie went to his room to get ready for the day. The house was quiet, as it usually was at this time of day. His mother was weaving at her table. He said goodbye to her and then headed off to his tutor.

As a Master Falconer, Charlie's father had the status in court in line with a junior commander in the King's Army. Nothing grand by any means, but not of the servant class either. His family lived a short distance from the castle instead of in the palace proper. They lived on Commander Row. It was a street about a five-minute walk from the main gates. His father's status gave them many benefits, but they were not allowed to attend any formal gatherings, except his father, of course. But then only those that required the presence of the King's falcons.

←→

"Charlie, good to see you." A smiling face greeted him at the door to the small single-room house where his tutor lived.

"Hi, Chadwick. Am I late?" Chadwick shook his head.

"No, I'm that early today. Master Erik couldn't believe his eyes when he saw me."

"I can imagine." Charlie's best friend, Chadwick, was always running late with one excuse or another.

After the other three boys arrived, they began their Reading, Mathematics, and Penmanship lessons. According to Master Erik, to become proper young men, they only needed those three skills.

When they were finally released for the day, Charlie and Chadwick took off at a run, heading to the castle mews. They spent every free moment there watching the apprentices and falconers care for and train the various falcons that it housed.

←→

The castle mews were the largest in the kingdom, they were told. Overall, it was able to house 30 falcons at any one time. The King's personal favorite was the Silver Gyrfalcon. They were only found in the most northern reaches of the Kingdom and were relatively rare. The King had five of them. No one else in the Kingdom was allowed to possess a Silver Gyrfalcon. The King's cousin Lord Alexander was said to have a Black Gyrfalcon, also quite rare, in his mews, but that might have only been a rumor.

When Queen Izabelle joined the King on a hunt, her falcon of choice was the Peregrine: a lethal falcon and the fastest flyer of all falcon species.

Prince William was Charlie's age and was now allowed to join the hunts. Since he was still young, his bird was a Merlin, one of the smallest of the falcons in the King's mews. Charlie loved all the different falcons that the castle housed.

At this time of day, the mews were quiet. All the birds were hooded and awaiting their turn in the practice yard.

"Charlie, look, the trappers have returned. Let's go see the new birds." Chadwick bounced with excitement. Several men entered the mews with large wooden crates. Nervous squawking and scratching could be heard coming from within the crates.

"You know that only the Falconers are allowed near the new birds; they don't want them any more scared than they already are. Come on, let's go see what the apprentices are doing today."

"Do you really think we will be selected?" Chadwick asked.

"My father told me this morning that I will become an apprentice next year."

Chadwick scoffed. "Of course, you will be selected. I can't imagine your own father not picking you. But what about me?"

"I'll see what I can do. I always just assumed you and I would be apprentices together." The two friends continued down the hallway that led from the mews to the practice yard.

If Charlie had to start at the bottom with all of the other apprentices, he needed to find out what they did. He had spent the whole day thinking about his apprenticeship.

Starting at the bottom was actually going to be the best thing for him. If he were given a top apprentice position, others would resent him for not earning his place. However, one thing was sure: he did not plan to stay on the bottom for long. He would do everything he could to advance on his merit and skill and not because of who his father was.

Chapter 2

The next few months were a blur in Charlie's memory. Before he knew it, Selection Day was upon him. His mother helped him dress in his finest clothes. It was still dark outside, but the eastern horizon was brightening. Charlie was excited beyond belief but still found himself yawning. His mother patted him on the behind and giggled at him.

Selection Day was the biggest day in a fourteen to seventeen-year-old boy's life. All trades used the same day to pick the next year's apprentices and squires, blacksmiths, horse trainers, military officers, potters, and jewelers, among others. However, in Charlie's opinion, Falconry was the most important trade and the only one worth doing. Boys from all over the Kingdom would meet at their town's central square at the crack of dawn and place their names in a bowl in front of the shield of their desired trade.

This was his first Selection Day as a fourteen-year-old. He could try again next year or pick a new trade if he was not chosen. He was eligible to keep trying until his seventeenth year. If he had not been selected by then, few choices were left. He didn't even want to think about not being chosen.

Charlie rushed out of the house. He wanted to be the first one at Castle Square. He didn't get to go to the square often, so this was a real treat. The trade shields were placed in a semi-circle in the center of the court. In front of each shield was a large copper bowl. Clutched tightly in his hand was a piece of parchment with his name written neatly on it. He raced to the Falconry Shield and deposited his name in the bowl without hesitation - the first one in.

He found a place to sit on the fountain's rim to wait. From this vantage spot, he could see all his competition.

⇇ ⇉

By the time the sun was above the horizon, the square was full of boys, their fathers milling around, and bowls full of names. The only ones allowed to view the selection were the fathers and the ones to be selected. No one else was allowed to be present. Charlie was highly nervous; he didn't really know what would happen today. He only knew that he would not see his mother until late tonight.

Charlie looked around for his friend Chadwick, late like usual.

Trumpets sounded, and everyone stopped moving and looked up at the Castle balcony overlooking the square. The balcony was at least three stories up. The King, Queen, and Prince appeared and walked to the railing. Charlie squinted his eyes, trying to make out their faces. They were so high up that he could only recognize the King. Charlie stood up on the fountain rim. The Selection was about to begin.

"Wait, don't start yet!!" Someone called from within the surrounding crowd. Charlie saw Chadwick racing for the bowls; he dropped his name in the Falconry bowl a split second before the cover was placed on top.

Chadwick looked at the guard holding the bowl. He smiled at the guard. The guard scowled at Chadwick but said nothing. Chadwick glanced up at the balcony and saw the King glaring at him. He gulped and slunk back into the crowd.

The King returned his gaze to survey the waiting crowd.

"Greetings to all, and welcome to Selection Day. An aspiring day for young boys and a proud one for fathers.

Today is the day that boys have the opportunity to try out for their desired trade." The King's voice boomed loudly and echoed through the square.

Murmurs erupted through the crowd from the youngest boys. *Try out. No one ever said this was a tryout,* Charlie thought to himself.

The King waited for the crowd to settle again. "That is correct. You all will try out against each other for the few positions available. Each trade will have a different number of apprentices chosen. The tryout process will take the entire day. The chosen will begin their training in the morning." There was a sea of grinning faces staring up at the King now. He smiled at the eager boys, then glanced at his son. The prince was standing with his arms crossed, and what appeared to be a sour expression was on his face. The Prince's long blonde hair covered his face when he shook it.

King Robert extended his hands to quiet the crowd. "For those of you at your first Selection, please do not think your new trade is secure. The Selection is only the first step. During your first and sometimes your second year, you are still being tested and can be released anytime. If you are not selected this year, you can try again next year for the same trade, or you are free to choose a different one.

"Please remember that your age today and how many times you have tried out matters not. You are equal and have the same chance of being selected. Good luck. I expect great things from those before me today." King Robert reached over to the bell beside him and struck it with his scepter. The King, Queen, and Prince departed. The King's herald approached the railing and roared for all to hear.

"Please approach the shield of your desired trade and follow your Selectors instructions."

Charlie looked back to where the Falconry Shield had been; all the shields had been moved. He looked around nervously. Where was the shield? He sighed with relief when he saw it a short distance from him. He walked over to the large crowd forming.

↞ ↠

It appeared that most of the fourteen-year-old boys wanted to become Falconers. The tryout must have been hard; few fifteen- and sixteen-year-olds were waiting. Charlie saw a boy that he knew who was sixteen.

"Hi, Alex. How many times have you tried out for Falconry?" He asked him.

"Oh, hi, Charlie. This is my third time. If I don't get chosen today, it will be my last time," he said sadly.

"How come?" He questioned.

"You'll find out. I'm not allowed to say." He said, shaking his head. Charlie struggled to swallow from a dry throat.

The Selector for Falconry was an aging man of about fifty. He looked at the zealous boys before him and cleared his raspy throat.

"I want you to divide yourselves into five equal groups." The twelve older boys broke off into three groups of four. The thirty younger boys looked around at each other. They were not used to such vague directions. How many are in each group? Should they group up with the older boys or start their own groups? Charlie could see the indecision written across their faces. Charlie did a quick headcount; there were 42 boys in all, and there was no way to make five equal groups. If they broke into five groups of eight, two would be left.

This is the first test, he thought. They could, however, divide into six groups of seven. Slowly, five groups formed, eight in four and nine in one other. Charlie had not joined a group. He squared his shoulders and took a deep breath; he hoped he was not doing the wrong thing. He approached the Selector. The old man looked at him.

"Is there a problem, young man?"

He swallowed loudly. "Yes, Sir. There is no way to make five equal groups, Sir. We can, however, make six groups of seven, Sir." He wrung his hands and then wiped them on his pants. He was sweating profusely. The Selector glared at him for a moment. Seeing that Charlie would not shy away from him, he nodded his head.

"This young man is correct. Divide into six groups of seven at once." Charlie jumped at the sharpness of the man's voice and ran back to the groups. The boys broke into six groups. Charlie found the one with only six members and joined that one, standing next to Chadwick. An apprentice Charlie had not seen before was taking notes. The Selector approached him and whispered something to him. The Apprentice nodded his head and wrote something down.

"You will go through a series of stations to see your abilities." One of the fourteen-year-olds raised his hand. "Yes?" The Selector said impatiently.

"Um, how can you test us? We have never done anything with birds before, and it doesn't seem fair."

"We want to see what we have to work with. This is not supposed to be fair. These tests will tell us how hard it will be to get you from what you are now to a falconer," he said with a scowl. The boy hid behind another boy to break his glare.

"Each group will complete one task and then move on to the next." Six Falconers approached to lead the groups to their first task. One group headed to the kennels, one to the mews, and the other four were taken to the practice yard.

←—→

Charlie's group was led to a cluster of tables with various leather straps. "Please select two jesses, two bells, and a leash for a Merlin. Younger boys go first," said the Falconer in front of them.

The younger boys look back and forth between themselves. Charlie heard one boy mutter, 'What is a Merlin?' Another boy shrugged his shoulders. Charlie and Chadwick stood behind the two other fourteen-year-olds in their group, allowing them to pick first. He knew exactly which ones to select. There were eight of the correct size and twelve different sizes that were all too large.

Once the two others chose their jesses, Charlie, Chadwick, and the older boys chose theirs. Charlie, Chadwick, another fourteen-year-old, and one older boy chose correctly. The Falconer wrote down their choices and placed their jesses, bells, and leashes in a pouch at his waist.

Their next challenge was making jesses of their own that would fit a Gyrfalcon. Each boy knew what a Gyrfalcon was and how big they were, but none knew how to make a jess. Charlie had watched his father make jesses countless times but had never honestly watched him complete each step. There was leather of different thicknesses and several different-shaped knives on the table before them. The boys selected a knife and some leather and began making what they thought would be a good jess. This task took a better part of an hour to complete. As they worked, there was no chatter; each boy was entirely focused on the task at hand.

They had to cut two thin strips of leather, attach a bell to it, and a ring for the leash.

When they had each completed their jess, they were allowed to rest under a tree before the next task began.

"So, how do you think you are doing?" One of the older boys asked Charlie.

"Well, I know I picked the correct jess for the Merlin, but I'm not sure my Gyrfalcon jess was right."

"Oh, good. I saw which jess you chose for the Merlin and copied you," the boy said.

Charlie smiled. He assumed most of them would.

"Why would you choose the same one like him?" One of the boys asked.

"Don't you know who he is?" The other boy shook his head no. "This is Master Kenton's son." The other boys' eyes opened wide with surprise and then narrowed.

"This is so unfair. Of course, he will be chosen."

"I am here trying out with the rest of you. I might have an advantage because I have been raised around falconry, but I still do not know everything. I have never made a jess before or seen it made from start to finish."

"But you knew what to expect coming into today, right?" He spat at him.

"I was as blind as the rest of you. I thought apprentices were just selected; I didn't know there was a tryout."

"He is right, Thaddeus. Everyone knows that the process of Selection Day is confidential. Until you have been through it, you are not permitted to know what goes on. Master Kenton is all too familiar with that law and would not betray our tradition even for his son." Trevor, their selection Falconer, said.

Thaddeus didn't say anything more on the subject but did not look convinced.

"Come now, time for your next task."

"How are we doing, Sir?" Thaddeus asked.

"I am not at liberty to say," Trevor replied. "Your next task will be a strength test. You will be hauling these logs from here across the field and then back until I say you are finished."

"Log pulling? What does that have to do with falconry?"

"Log pulling itself? Absolutely nothing. What we are doing is seeing your upper body strength. Carrying a falcon on your fist all day can be quite tiring. Now begin."

All the logs appeared to be about the same size. Charlie grabbed a rope attached to one of the logs and started to pull. The log slowly slid along the ground. At first, all the boys were dragging their logs relatively evenly. The return trip began showing gaps between the older and younger boys. *The older boys that had been through this before had most likely trained during the year leading up to Selection Day,* Charlie thought to himself glumly. He lowered his stance and dug his feet into the ground. The log kept moving. Trevor stood at the starting line with his arms crossed. The first boy's back stopped, breathing heavily. Trevor shook his head and pointed back down the field.

Groaning, the boys picked up their ropes and returned the other way. After five complete trips, Trevor finally allowed them to stop. All the boys collapsed to the ground. Charlie looked at his hands; they had cracked open in a couple of places and were bleeding. He looked at the others and noticed several looking at their hands.

"I'm so glad we did the log pull after making our jesses," Charlie said aloud. A couple of the others laughed.

"I couldn't hold a knife now even if my life depended on it," Chadwick replied.

"On your feet," Trevor roared.

"Can't we rest for a moment?" Thaddeus asked. Trevor did not reply. He turned and started walking toward the kennels. All of them moaning and some whimpering, the boys got to their feet and slowly plodded after Trevor.

←→

The walk to the kennels was short. But even before they reached the entrance door, the dogs inside could be heard yipping and barking. The kennel had several types of dogs depending on the kind of quarry that would be hunted. The falconers mostly used pointers and flushers, but other dogs were also in the kennels. Hounds were used for foxhunting, and retrievers were used for archery bird hunting.

"We are going to see how well you handle the dogs. Each of you will be teamed with a dog. Your job is to get them through an obstacle course. Please step forward and receive your dog."

Charlie stepped forward first. He was handed the leash to a small, long-bodied flusher. She wagged her tail at him. She had a long-pointed nose and long ears. Trevor led him to the starting line of the obstacle course. The other boys stayed behind. There would be no advantages in seeing the course layout ahead of time.

Charlie's dog's leash was removed, and he was instructed to begin. The course was a series of logs to go over, under, and through. Charlie had never worked with a dog before and didn't know the commands. He jogged up to the first log; it looked like they needed to go over it.

"Ok, girl, up and over," he said, pointing over the log. The dog looked up at him with her tongue dangling out of her mouth. Charlie sighed. *How do I get the dog to understand what I want without the proper command?* He thought. "Come on, girl, come here." He patted his hands on his legs. The dog took a step over to him. *Well, that's one way.*

Charlie walked to the log and climbed over it, calling her to him. She scrambled up the log and nimbly jumped off. One log down, many to go. Charlie went through the course, up logs, under logs, and through logs, with the dog following closely behind. He came to the final log; it was too small for him to fit through. He told the dog to sit and stay at the log's opening. He jogged over to the other end. He got down on all fours and looked through the log. "Girl, come here, girl. Where is she?" He said. "Girl, come here." He heard the dog bark at him. She was sitting next to him. She went the same way he did, not through the log.

He led her back to the other side and had her sit again. He tried it one more time. He only had three tries to get her through the log before they told him to continue. He called her, and once again, he found her beside him. Only one more chance. He led her to the other side once more. "Let's try this differently. Girl, come here." He patted the opening of the log. The dog moved over and glanced inside. "Ok, so far, so good. What is the command?" He pondered for a moment. He patted the opening again and said, "Flush." The dog took off at a sprint into the log. He jumped for joy and then ran to the other side. The dog emerged triumphantly with a rabbit hide in her mouth and then shook her head back and forth.

An apprentice approached, reattached the leash to her collar, and led her off.

Trevor stood off to the side, writing down his notes. "Please wait over there and do not speak," he said.

Charlie walked to the designated spot and sat on the grass to watch the others get their dogs through the course.

Some boys did better than others, but they all got their dogs through the course.

"One more task to complete. To the mews, please," Trevor requested.

The boys jumped to their feet, finally the part they had been waiting for. The whole purpose of being a falconer was to be near the falcons.

"This is bird identification. I know most of you have not been allowed near the birds before, so I will be going over a key feature of each bird species housed here, and then I will take you into the mews one by one and have you identify the birds for me."

One by one, the boys entered the mews and exited out another door. Charlie was the last to enter. The birds in the mews were grouped by size: Merlins and Kestrels together, Prairies were next, and then the Peregrines. The final birds housed in their own separate section of the mews were the Kingdom's pride and joy, the Gyrfalcons. Charlie named off each species as they passed them and then froze in awe at the Gyrfalcons. He had seen them many times before, but their beauty still struck him each time.

"Beautiful birds, aren't they?"

"Yes, Sir!" Charlie exclaimed.

"Thank you for trying out today. You are dismissed," Trevor said.

"When will we find out if we made it?"

"How many of us will be chosen?"

"How did we do?"

Questions came flying in all at once. Trevor held up his hand. "Your fathers will be contacted in the morning. Get some sleep; those chosen will need it."

Charlie and Chadwick walked out together into the main square. Chadwick's' father was near the fountain, speaking with several other fathers.

"How did it go, boys?" He asked with a grin.

"Nothing like I expected," Chadwick said.

"I've never tried out for Falconry, but I've heard it is no harder or easier than smithing," Chadwick's father said.

"How many times did you have to try out?" Charlie asked.

"Twice, but I tried out for the Squires first. I figured I didn't have what it took to be a knight, so I might be better at making the weapons. I was right."

"Oh... I wish we would have been told all of this before," Chadwick whined.

His father patted him on the back, "Where's the fun in that? Come on. Your mom's waiting for us."

"Bye, Charlie."

"Bye, Chadwick."

Charlie waved goodbye. After a few moments, he returned to the mews to see if his father was ready to head home. He turned his gaze to the king's box. Prince William was there staring down at him with a scowl on his face.

Charlie stared back and then smiled and waved. The prince's facial features changed to one of confusion. After a few breaths, he slowly raised his hand in a tentative wave with a shy smile. Charlie waved again and then hurried to the mews.

Chapter 3

The following morning, Charlie wakes to find his father gone. He was sure he would be there to tell him if he was chosen or not. Well, maybe this was his way of telling him. Charlie shuffled out the door. Even his mother had left earlier than usual for the market.

The first day of the week, Market Day, was always busy. Only market stalls were open on Market Day, and most businesses and all schools were closed.

Charlie wound his way through the stalls, looking for his mother. She was nowhere to be seen. *Must have missed her*, he thought to himself. He stopped at a baker's stall, bought a couple of muffins, and headed home slowly.

He hesitated at the front door. What would he do? How could he face anyone he knew? The son of the Head Falconer couldn't make it; could he stomach trying again?

He let out a deep, long sigh, squared his shoulders, and opened the door. He stopped and listened; no one was home. Where could they be? He walked the short distance to the kitchen table; a small package was in the center. That wasn't there when he left; he was sure of that. He saw his name written neatly on the top in his father's script. He reached for the package, his hands shaking slightly. Carefully, he unwrapped it to reveal an apprentice's leather tunic. He picked it up and sat heavily in a chair.

He made it; he really did it. Was it his doing, or did his father pull strings? No, his father wouldn't do that. He stared at the tunic, rubbing his thumbs across the smooth, soft leather. Suddenly, his eyes snapped to the door as his mind raced. Chadwick, did he make it? He jumped up and rushed out the door with his new tunic clutched tightly in his hand.

He ran through the streets, taking a shortcut through an ally he knew well. Numerous pigeons took flight in the wake of his mad dash to Chadwick's house. Chadwick was sitting outside playing a game with his little sister. Charlie slid to a halt in front of them. Chadwick looked up at his friend.

"So, did you make it?" He asked him. Charlie nodded, completely out of breath. "I knew you would. I just wanted to be there with you," he said sadly. Chadwick's sister glanced between them, mumbled something, and then entered their house.

Charlie opened his mouth but snapped it shut; he didn't know what to say, so he sat next to his friend instead.

They sat in silence for a few minutes. "Don't feel bad for me. Just think about it; I get an entire year off. No tutor, no apprenticeship, just lazing around the house."

Charlie laughed softly, "Like your mom will let that happen."

Chadwick ran his hands through his red hair and chuckled, "Yay."

A few more moments of silence passed.

"Will you try again next year?" Charlie asked.

He sighed, "I don't know. I know what to expect now, but my uncle visited this morning and told me what he did." He paused.

"Well, what did he do?"

"He tried out for two different things and then picked one to work toward for the third year—it kind of makes sense. I don't know if Falconry is what I want to do forever. I know I don't want to be a smithy," he shook his head. "My dad loves it and has taken me with him a couple of times, but that is not my life.”

“What would you try for next year?”

“I’m not sure. My uncle said to spend this year watching the other trades. See what they do, ask questions, learn, and then decide.”

“Sounds like a good idea.” Charlie frowned, “Maybe that is what they should tell all of us a couple of months before our first selection day.”

Chadwick smiled, “Well, to quote my father, ‘Where’s the fun in that.’”

↞ ↠

Charlie hugged his mom again. He knew that he would eventually have to move into The House, but he didn’t think it would be so soon. The House was like the barracks for the falconers. His mom smoothed his hair down again. “Mom...” he whined softly, “It’s not like we will never see each other again. I’ll be home every break I get.”

“Every mother hears those words; don’t make promises you are too young to keep,” she said with a sad smile.

He nodded.

“You have everything I packed for you?”

“Yes, ma’am.”

“Good. Now, chin up. You will do well. You will be the next Head Falconer. I know it.”

He swallowed heavily and nodded again.

His father was again absent as he walked to his new home. It was a relatively short walk. His father was not allowed to live too far away from his charges.

The House was behind the mews, out of sight from most of the Castle but close enough for the falconers to be available at a moment's notice.

A small, well-worn path led to the front door. Several other boys were walking up the path in front of him. *How many made it*, he wondered.

"Welcome, First-Years." They were greeted by Trevor from Selection Day. "We will wait here for the last two to arrive."

Charlie glanced around; Alex was there, and they shared a quick smile. There were four other boys he didn't know.

"Hurry up, Thaddeus. You're late!" Trevor shouted.

Charlie's head whipped around. Thaddeus had made it? How was that possible?

"All right, everyone this way."

"I thought you said we were waiting for two more?"

"This way." He repeated. He led them through the entry hall into the main common area. "The Castle's kitchen will be where you eat all your meals for the first year. There are no exceptions unless you have a day off, which will be few and far apart. You may bring your food back here if you wish, though. You will have set wake-up, meal, work, and lights-out times for your first year, with no exceptions and no variations. Your first year will be boring, and your fingers will hurt. In your second year, you will wish for boring and hurt fingers. You have all been assigned a roommate; no switching is allowed. Alex and Tad, Malick and Lance, Morty and Thaddeus, Charlie and Wesley."

Charlie exhaled the breath he didn't realize he was holding; he wasn't placed with Thaddeus. But who was Wesley?

"This way to your rooms."

Charlie was given the first room. He entered and closed the door. Inside the small space was a window in the middle, a bed on each side, one table under it with two chairs, and a small chest at the foot of each bed. There were two red shirts to wear under his leather tunic and an envelope near the pillow.

He placed his bag on one of the chests and sat down. Inside the envelope, he found his itinerary for the week. There was nothing on the list for the rest of the day until after dinner.

The door opened, and a boy walked in; he had his gaze on the floor in front of him. He closed the door behind him and threw his bag on the bed. He looked up and jumped in surprise to see Charlie sitting there.

"I'm sorry, I thought I, uh, I mean, I thought we had private rooms."

"So, did I. I'm Charlie. You must be Wesley?"

"Wesley? Yay, right, I'm Wesley." He said nervously. He tossed his head to one side like he was tossing hair out of his eyes, but his hair was cropped short and didn't budge. Wesley reached up and scratched his head before walking the short distance to the empty bed.

"I've never seen you around here before. Where are you from?"

"I'm from a small hamlet far to the north called Northron." He stammered. "Our Falconer died in an accident, so they sent me here. The King agreed to allow me to join your class, and after I complete my training, I will return to my hamlet and take up the role of Master." He sat on the bed across from Charlie.

"Those are big shoes to fill."

"Tell me about it."

"Well, since you are new here, how about a tour? I'm not sure where everything is, but I know how to get to the mews."

"Sure, thanks."

Charlie smiled and led him out of their room to give him a tour of the mews and as much of the Castle as he was allowed to go.

↞ ↠

After dinner, the eight first years met in the common room. Trevor was again there to greet them.

"Hope your first day was relaxing. Tomorrow won't be. Your first few weeks will be spent in the classroom. It will be a lot of learning in very little time. Do not waste time thinking that the book information is not important. Remember, you can be released from the program at any time."

"What's after the classroom?" Thaddeus asked.

Trevor rolled his eyes, "Equipment maintenance. Now off to bed; the first bell is early."

Chapter 4

Trevor was right about the first couple of weeks. They were thrown a whirlwind of information, from the founding of their kingdom and the Royal Falconer Court to the types of birds, dogs, and training techniques. They also learned how the first nobles of Weshingham had chosen their first King through a falconry competition.

Lance and Morty visibly struggled since they never attended a formal school. Alex, being the eldest, seemed to fly right through the coursework and spent his extra time coaching them. Tad, Thaddeus, and Malick stuck together all the time. Wesley sat apart whenever possible and never spoke unless spoken to. Charlie tried to engage him in conversation several times during his free time but was shrugged off each time.

So, Charlie sat alone most of the time. He didn't mind too much. He concentrated on his studies, and by the time coursework was set to end, he felt confident he would pass the exam with high marks.

On the exam day, they were awoken by panicked banging on their door. Charlie and Wesley bolted out of bed and rushed to the door together. Wesley reached the door a step faster and threw it open; four men with masks rushed in and tackled them to the floor, tied their hands behind their backs, roughly gaged them, and threw a hood over their heads. They were forced to stand and then they were pushed into the hallway. Charlie and Wesley shouted at their attackers and tried to fight as best as possible. Charlie could hear the other dorm room doors being thrown open and the other apprentices treated the same. Standing back-to-back with Wesley, Charlie recognized Trevor's voice. Charlie felt the tension leave Wesley's back like a tidal wave.

When all the apprentices were in the hallway, a rough voice told them to march. They were ushered a short distance and then told to sit. Hands grabbed his shoulders and forced him down into a chair. After what seemed like an eternity, the bindings around his wrists were cut, and the hood yanked off his head. He blinked several times at the sudden brightness as he tried to pull the gag out of his mouth. He looked around at their classroom. Several teachers sat at the front of the room, and several other Falconers stood around the room's edges. He looked down at his desk, and as he suspected, his test was there.

"You may begin. No talking, no questions." Trevor said from somewhere behind him.

As one, the apprentices began their test. After about an hour, stomachs could be heard growling throughout the classroom. Another hour passed, and Charlie sighed and quickly thumbed through the book before him. *How long is this test?* He thought.

Finally, after another hour, Alex stood and walked his exam to the front of the room. A few minutes later, Charlie and Wesley stood at the same time. Tad was a few steps behind them. They exited the classroom; Alex was still there in the hallway.

"What the hell was that?" Alex exclaimed.

"I don't know; I thought I was being abducted," Tad said.

"Me too, not that it would do them any good," Alex said. "My parents have nothing to which to pay a ransom with."

"I'm starving. Can we go eat, or do we have to stay here?" Tad asked.

"Well, they didn't say not to; let's go to the kitchen and see if there is anything left to eat," Alex replied.

Charlie and Wesley glanced at each other and shrugged simultaneously as they fell into step with the other two boys.

Delicious scents reached their noses before they rounded the corner and entered the kitchen.

"I'm glad the kitchen staff knew about our late appearance at breakfast." Charlie sighed happily. The serving table was loaded with a wide assortment of pastries, meats, and cheeses.

Each boy loaded their plate high and found a table to sit at. Wesley started to veer to a different table. "Sit with us, Wesley. We won't bite," Alex told him. He stared at the older boy for a moment before joining them.

They ate in silence and waited for the other four boys to join them.

"Congrats, boys, you all passed." Trevor greeted them with a smile.

A couple of nods and scowls greeted him, "Come on, it wasn't that bad; I went through it."

"I only have one question… why?" Thaddeus asked.

"Well, it's simple." Trevor sat down at the table. "All of you come from less than Noble Families. Charlie, here, is from the highest standing, but only because of his father's hard-won status. None of you have been around Royalty, and you do not know the fickleness of Nobles. When you become a full Falconer, especially you, Wesley, as the only Falconer in your hamlet, when they decide it is time for a hunt, it is time to go."

"In the middle of the night?" Morty whined.

"Sometimes. I was once awoken at midnight and told to gather the birds and dogs. We rode till daybreak, hunted for a few hours, and then collapsed by the fire when we finally were allowed to. The Lord was fighting with his Lady and needed to get away. We were kept out there for four days before we returned. You have to be prepared for anything. That exam today was easy, but taking that exam with your nerves rattled, all eyes staring at you, hunger pains distracting you, that was the actual test. Could you concentrate and do what you needed to do?

"You are being trained to handle birds, but in all truth, you are the only thing that will keep those birds alive. Your Noble has no care for their lives, only their own pleasure. Whenever you go on extended trips, always take more than one bird. You will keep several birds that look alike; most Nobles do not notice the nuanced differences between the birds and will not know when you switch one out for another.

"Now, go and relax. You have the rest of the day off."

All eight boys grinned as one. This was their first free day. Trevor smiled as all the boys jumped up and rushed back to their rooms to change. He didn't expect to see any of them again until lights out.

↞ ↠

Charlie rushed into his room and changed his clothes as quickly as possible. His first stop was to see his mother and then Chadwick. As he bolted out of the door, he collided with Wesley. They fell into a heap on the floor.

"Sorry, oh, I am so sorry. Here, let me help you up," Charlie said.

"It's okay, really, I'm fine. Big day planned?"

"Going to visit my mother and my best friend." He hesitated. Wesley didn't know anyone in town, "Do you want to join me?"

Wesley's eyes opened wide, "Why?"

Charlie shuffled his feet, "Well, I don't know, you don't know anyone in town, won't be much fun by yourself, that's all." He rambled.

"Oh, well, that is very kind of you." He paused, "I'll be fine; go see your family. I'll see you tonight." Wesley entered their room and shut the door.

Charlie shrugged and hurried down the hallway.

He burst through the front door to his family's home. "Mother, I'm home!" He called.

"Charlie, is that you?" His mother answered from her sewing room. "Oh, my boy, so glad you're home. It's a free day, right?"

"Yes, mama. I didn't get dismissed," he scoffed.

She ruffled his hair, "I didn't think so."

"We took our first exam today, and then they gave us the rest of the day off."

"How did you do?"

He shrugged, "They just said we all passed."

"Well, that's good; I don't want any of you being dismissed. Are you hungry?"

"No, I ate just before coming. How is everything around here?" They spent the next hour catching up on the local gossip before his mother stood and said she needed to get back to work. Charlie kissed his mother's cheek and went to find Chadwick.

Would he be at school or working somewhere?

Chadwick's mother was home with his little sister. He was told Chadwick was at the smithy with his father.

That's funny. That is the last place I expected to find him; he hates that place.

The smithy was near the Castle but opposite from the Mews.

Charlie peered into the window and squinted his eyes as his face was assaulted by hot air billowing through the open window. Chadwick's father and the other two smithies working that day were hammering away at various things; Charlie couldn't tell exactly what they were working on. A couple of Journeymen were sharpening what looked to be a sword and a couple of axes. Three apprentices were working the bellows. He strained his neck, trying to see inside more. Finally, he spotted Chadwick stacking swords and other weapons in a corner.

Not wanting to interrupt, he went to the well in front of the shop, took a sip of water, and then found a shaded spot to sit and wait. He drifted off at some point but jolted awake when someone kicked his foot slightly. He snapped his eyes open to see Chadwick smiling down at him.

"What are you doing here? Don't tell me you got kicked out?" He laughed.

Charlie held out his hand; his friend grabbed his wrist and helped him to his feet. "Of course not. I got the day off, that's all. What are you doing here?"

"My dad's doing."

"Are you an apprentice?"

Chadwick shook his head, "No worse, free labor." He chuckled, "Getting an unfair advantage, so I am told more than once a day."

"By whom?"

"The apprentices and Journeymen. I have no desire to do that," he pointed behind him, "every day for the rest of my life. I would rather feed the pigs."

"Really, that bad?" Pig farming did not attract recruits; farms were usually handed down from father to son.

He chuckled again, "No, not that bad. Come on; I have a few minutes to eat. Hungry?"

Charlie looked up at the sky and saw that the sun was high overhead; he didn't have much time left of his free day. "I can eat, come on."

"So, how is everything?" Charlie asked.

Chadwick shrugged; his face looked clouded with a far-off look, "Same as always, I guess."

"Well, something seems off with you."

Chadwick grinned slightly, "You know we always have enough; my father's status ensures we are cared for. But in my free time, I've seen things I've never known. The other day, I went walking. I wasn't paying attention to where I was going and found myself in the Burrows."

"The Burrows? Never been over there before."

"I don't recommend it either. Life there is drastically different."

"How so?"

"Well, I guess I didn't notice anything at first. Shopkeepers sweeping out their storefronts, shoppers going from store to store. But then I started to actually look at the people. They looked thinner, their eyes dim. I still saw kids running around and playing in the alleys, but their clothes weren't more than rags, and most were barefoot."

"Well, maybe they save their finer clothing for special days."

"I thought so as well. On my next day off, I went back, though."

Charlie stared at his friend with his mouth agape. "Why?" was all that came out.

Chadwick shrugged, "I don't know. Something felt off. I saw a girl and tried to strike up a conversation."

"Did it work?"

"Not a first. I went back every night for a week before she finally spoke to me." He sighed deeply, "Our city might as well be two for how different they are governed." Charlie gave him a questioning look, his eyes begging him to continue. "People that live in the Burrows are primarily poor. None of the tradesmen that Mariann knows have contracts with the King or any noble, for that matter. She and her older brother assumed the King had all his tradesmen living within the Castle. They didn't realize that we lived so differently."

Charlie thought for a moment. "Well, I guess not everyone can sell to the King. But why did everyone look so thin?"

"I asked them about that. They said food has been scarce."

"What? I don't see any signs of that."

"They say that lately, their Giving Day has been suspended."

Charlie's eyes went wide. "What is the Giving Day?"

"Giving Day is normally once every other week. Everyone is given staples of flour, eggs, and sugar. Sometimes, meat was given. I asked my father about it. He said that was none of my business and forbade me from ever returning there again."

"I, I don't know what to say."

Chadwick shrugged, "All I know is life is not as it seems."

Before Charlie could formulate another question, Chadwick had to return. Charlie said goodbye, promising to see him again on his next free day. Hopefully, Chadwick would have the day off as well.

←→

Charlie walked through the market before making his way back to The House, contemplating what Chadwick had told him and trying to make sense of it. The main room was empty, as were the apprentice dorms; all the doors were open while a couple of ladies went from room to room, changing the bedding and general cleaning, he assumed. Not wanting to interrupt them, he went to the courtyard.

He walked toward the center tree, grabbed an apple from another tree as he passed it, and sat on the ground, leaning against it. He closed his eyes and soon drifted off.

Chapter 5

Wesley closed the door on Charlie. *Why is father forcing me to go through this*? He stalked to his chest and rummaged through it to find the carefully wrapped bundle he hid in the bottom. He placed the bundle into his bag. Slinging his pack over his shoulder, he quickly left The House and headed to the Castle kitchen.

He walked through the servants' corridors with his head down, looking at no one but pretending he was supposed to be there. Several kitchen staff and one guard passed him, but no one gave him a second look.

He entered the Hall of Portraits, empty as usual. He quickly walked down the hallway, cringing at the loud echoes of his boots on the polished marble flooring. He stole glances at all the past Kings as he walked, each holding their preferred Bird of Prey. Next to most of the large portraits was a smaller one showing the Queen; a few had more than one Queen when one had passed before their husband. He reached the end of the hall where the current king's portrait was always placed and looked around. He grabbed ahold of the picture frame and, with a slight grunt, moved the picture on slightly stiff hinges. The opening behind the picture was only known to a few. He slipped into the opening and pulled the picture closed behind him.

He stood there momentarily to give his eyes time to adjust to the darkness and ensure no one saw him. He fumbled in the dark for a small light switch. A small bulb bloomed to life, giving the small hole a soft glow. He knew the light would be hidden behind the picture. After digging through his bag momentarily, he pulled out a large key. The key was the perfect match for the lock on the door. The lock opened with a soft click, and he walked into a long, narrow hallway. Flicking off one light and flicking on another, he closed the door and locked it again before running as quickly as he could down the narrow space.

Reaching the end of the hallway, another door greeted him. This one was never locked. He opened it and peered into the room, empty. He let out the breath he was holding, entered, and closed the door, leaning on it heavily. He tossed his bag onto a chair next to the cold fireplace. He strolled through the room, the prince's room. He dragged his hand across the comforter on the bed and fluffed up a pillow slightly. The armoire door was slightly ajar. He went to it and pulled the door fully open. The mirror on the door showed a rag-tag-looking boy with hair cut way too short and a face bunched in a frown and far too dirty. He picked out a clean shirt, breaches, shiny knee-high boots, and a waistcoat and tossed them on the bed. He looked at the bathroom; it wouldn't hurt, he mused.

The Castle was one of the few buildings in the Kingdom with electricity, running water, and running hot water.

He drew himself a bath, peeled off his apprentice clothing, and slid into the steamy water with a groan of pleasure and relief. He sat for a moment but didn't dally too long and was soon dressed in clothing finer than he had been allowed to wear in what seemed ages.

He grabbed his bag again and fished out a ring, which he placed on his right ring finger. Looking in the mirror one more time, he grinned and nodded to his reflection.

Now, to do what he came here for. He flung open the main door to the prince's room and walked briskly out. The guard beside the door straightened and saluted as he walked by.

"I didn't know you had returned, your Highness," he said as he fell in step with him.

Wesley smiled but didn't reply.

"Where is he?" Wesley asked after a moment.

"His Majesty is in his private study, Sir."

Wesley nodded.

When they reached the King's study, the guards saluted and knocked on the door. A muffled reply came from within. "Prince William here to see you, Sire." The guard said in return and then opened the door.

"William, my boy, so good of you to come on your day off."

"It's Wesley, remember?" He scowled.

King Robert smiled, "Of course, Wesley. So, how is the apprenticeship going?"

"It is just dreadful, father. Remind me again why you are forcing me to do this?"

"It will make sense, trust me. Every prince has entered an apprenticeship in secret at your age."

"But why Falconry? Shouldn't I be doing something that will help me run the country? Like being a Knight or something?"

King Robert shook his head, "No Falconry will do." William crossed his arms and stomped his foot. "Now, now. It is only for a few short years."

"Years??" William's mouth dropped. "I thought you would recall me any day. What will people think if the crown prince is missing for years?"

"You don't give me much credit. You are going to the finest University in Northron, don't you know."

"University? Father, what will the court say when I return from this University in a couple of years? No smarter than I am now because, let me tell you, I will not be getting any smarter around those commoners."

"Watch your behavior, son. Those commoners are your subjects. You will learn more than you realize if you open your eyes and mind. Watch them, study them, and get to know them." King Robert dropped his eyes to his reports.

"Get to know them? You want me to make friends?"

King Robert glanced up and smiled, "Making a few true friends will come in handy, trust me."

"What do you mean, true friends?"

"Come now, do you really think the boys you call friends from the court are friendly to you just because they like you?" He held up his hand, "I know a few of them do, but trust me, if times changed and you were no longer the crown prince, many would abandon you quicker than you can blink. But when you can make a friend when they do not know your true origins, you know you have a true friend that will stick with you.

"Now I have kingly things to see to. Off with you."

"I will return on my next free day. Tell Mother I will see her then."

"No."

"What?"

"You will not return until Summer Festival."

"Summer Festival is almost a year away."

"Yes, and that is when the University sends students home on break."

"But I am not at the University; why can't I come home? No one saw me. I wish to see mother."

"She believes you are at the University and will continue to believe it. If you wish to write her, send the letter to me, and I will deliver it for you. Now go, become a Falconer."

William hung his head, "Yes, sir." He turned to leave.

"I'm proud of you, son." King Robert whispered.

"Thank you, Father." He whispered back and left the room.

He walked back to his room slowly. He changed his clothing and then sat on his bed. He looked around one last time; it would be months before he returned.

↞ ↠

Charlie was startled awake when someone passed by him. "Wesley! Hi!" He said cheerfully.

Wesley jumped and spun around, "Sorry, I didn't see you there."

"What time is it?" Charlie asked, stifling a yawn.

"Almost dinner bell, I think."

"Want to grab a bite together?"

"Sure." He shrugged, "Let me drop my bag off first."

"Ok, I'll walk with you." Charlie fell in stride with Wesley as they silently walked back to their room.

"Hey guys, wait up," Alex called, running down the hallway. "Did you hear?"

"Hear what?" Charlie asked.

"A couple of the fourth years will be free-flying their new birds for the first time; want to go watch?"

"Well... yes. Can we grab some dinner first?" Charlie smiled broadly. The first free flight was crucial in the training phase, and sometimes they didn't return.

"That's where I'm going; come on, let's hurry."

They rushed to the kitchen, piled up a plate high with meat, cheese, and biscuits, and then hurried out to the training yard. They found a quiet spot under a tree to watch the show.

Three falconers wearing the tunic of a fourth-year came out of the Mews with hooded birds on their fists. The fourth-years were glowing with excitement. Master Kenton walked out behind them.

One of the apprentice falconers walked in front of the others. He placed his bird on a perch and removed its hood.

"What kind is that? We are too far away." Alex said.

"Peregrine," Charlie answered.

The falconer walked about 10 feet away, fished something out of his pocket, and placed it on his glove. He raised his glove and whistled. His bird ruffled its feathers and looked around. He raised his glove again and whistled. On the third attempt, his bird flew to the glove and took the tidbit of meat. The apprentice smiled and walked back to the perch. He messed around with the bird's leg momentarily and then walked 20 feet away.

"What did he do to its leg?" Wesley asked.

"A thin string is attached to his leg in case it didn't fly to him. Now is the true test."

The apprentice repeated his motions, raising his glove with what looked like an entire rabbit on it, and whistled. He only had to ask twice that time. His falcon flew true, soaring through the air, gliding low over the grass, and raising to land on the glove at the last moment. The falcon grabbed ahold of the rabbit tightly and tried to fly off with it. The falconer kept a tight hold of the rabbit and quickly gathered up the jesses to keep the bird there.

"Good, good, next," Master Kenton shouted.

The next apprentice approached and went through the same motions; his bird was a little more corporative and got his reward quicker.

The third and final apprentice didn't have as much luck. While the leash was attached, his bird flew to the fist on its first presentation of the glove. Master Kenton asked the young falconer if he should try one more time or go free-flight. The falconer elected to go free-flight. His bird sat calmly on the perch and looked around. The apprentice grabbed the rabbit as the others did; his bird ignored the whistle and started to preen its feathers. The apprentice whistled again and shook the rabbit in his glove. His bird perked up and shook itself before taking off, gliding straight to his handler before veering at the last second, climbing into the air, and circling the training yard.

The training yard was covered with a large net to keep birds like this one from getting too far away. The bird flew a couple of circles before finding a spot to land.

Master Kenton shook his head and approached the apprentice, saying something to him that Charlie couldn't hear, but when Kenton and the other two left, he guessed it was you get to stay here until it comes to you. The errant bird's handler approached the bird and continued to call to it.

"How long do you think it will be?" Alex asked.

Charlie shrugged, "Not sure. When the bird gets hungry enough, it will come down. Shouldn't be too long, though."

"Why is that?" Wesley asked.

Charlie and Alex shared a glance. "In order to hunt and cooperate, the birds have to be a little hungry," Charlie said.

Wesley's mouth dropped open, "What? That is cruel!" He exclaimed.

"He said hungry, not starving. A full bird doesn't hunt; a full bird doesn't listen. Haven't you ever watched your town's falconers before?" Alex asked him.

Wesley's face paled, "Um, um..." He trailed, "We only had the one for the longest time; he was a very secretive person. He never let people see him work out the birds and only had two other falconers with him. This was the first year he tried out an apprentice in years, and he only picked one." He kept his eyes downcast as he spoke.

"Wow, tough place. Well, I'm glad you can be here then," Alex said warmly.

Wesley looked up and grinned.

Charlie's thoughts return to his conversation with Chadwick earlier in the day. *Why did this conversation bring me back to that one?*

They sat in silence, watching the apprentice try to call his bird over and over again until boredom took them, and they retired for the night.

Chapter 6

The days came and went with a steady, monotonous rhythm. After they learned how to repair equipment and care for the dogs, they were placed into the rotation doing just that.

Charlie, Wesley, and Alex spent all their free time together in the mews whenever possible. Charlie taught the others all he knew about the birds: their favorite quarry, where they came from, and the best methods on how to use them. On their days off, they would follow any falconers exercising their birds beyond the training yards.

"I'm so glad you are my friend," Alex said to Charlie one day.

Charlie stopped scrubbing a bath pan and looked up, "What?" He asked, confused.

"I'm just glad we are friends, that's all." Alex shrugged.

"Why is that?" Charlie wiped the sweat off his brow with the back of his hand.

"You are a wealth of knowledge."

"Well, I don't know about that."

"Don't discount yourself so quickly. Yesterday, one of the birds got loose in the training yard. The Falconer grabbed a fox that had just been brought in, tied a rope to it, and threw it up. The falcon just looked at the fox and started to preen. I grabbed a quail, tied a string to it, and threw it out. The falcon took flight immediately and sailed down. The falconer glared at me, but Master Kenton was watching and nodded to me. Before you taught me so much, I assumed meat was meat. Without you, I wouldn't have caught the Master's eye. Thank you," Alex said sincerely.

Charlie's cheeks warmed, "You're welcome. I love telling people about the birds; I've never had someone so willing to listen."

"What about that friend of yours?"

"Chadwick? Oh, he listened for a while but never cared as much as me."

"Well, when you want to talk, I'm all ears." Alex smiled.

⇜ ⇝

Alex ran down the dorm hallway, skidding to a halt in front of Charlie and Wesley's room; he threw open the door, causing both boys to jump to their feet.

"What's the meaning of that?" Charlie yelled.

Alex panted, trying to catch his breath, "Sorry... I... I..." He tried to speak.

"Calm down and spit it out already," Wesley said.

"I have news." He managed.

"Well, what is it?" Wesley asked impatiently.

"The King is going on a hunt, and they are taking all the birds; everyone is going, even us."

Wesley stood, "What do you mean even us?" His face paled.

"Well, I was cleaning up the dog run, and the King came in; seeing him up so close was amazing. He told Master Kenton to prepare a hunt. Master Kenton said it would be done. The King left; he didn't even look at me, but then why would he? Master Kenton was about to leave, then looked over at me. He said to pick two friends and join the hunt. Isn't it great that we get to go on a Royal Hunt as first-years?"

"I don't... I don't want to go," Wesley stammered.

"How can you say that?" Charlie exclaimed.

Wesley shrugged.

"Come on, my two best friends must come with me," Alex said.

Wesley looked up, "Best friend?"

Alex slapped him on the back, "Of course. Now you have to come with Charlie and me."

He looked between the two boys, his friends. Boys who liked him because of who he was, not who his father was. They didn't even know the truth of who he really was. Would they still like him if they knew? "Okay, I'll go."

"Great, better getting packing; we leave at sun-up."

The city street was lined with people as The Royal Procession traveled slowly out of the city into the countryside. The King and his top advisors led the group atop their spirited horses, followed by Master Kenton carrying the King's Gyrfalcon and four additional falconers on foot with various birds on their fists. The dogs and their handlers were next, followed by the support staff with the wagons of tents, food, and supplies. Alex, Charlie, and Wesley were the last in line. They walked next to the Mews Cart. Ten additional birds were housed inside.

"I bet Prince William will be sad to miss this hunt. I hear that he loves the hunt," Alex said.

"Who told you that?" Wesley asked.

"Oh, just talk that I heard. But who wouldn't love this? I am so excited to be invited to join this."

"Me too. I always wished my father could take me with him. This is the best day of my life." Charlie remarked.

Wesley shook his head with a smile. His new friends had simple desires and simple expectations. He was slowly starting to envy their lives. Their pressures were few, and their free time was always theirs.

Once outside the main city gates, the falconers carrying birds placed them inside the Mews Cart and mounted their horses.

The apprentices were left to climb into the Mews Cart. They wiggled down on the floor between the large crates the birds rode in. Soon, the boys nodded off one by one, lulled to sleep by the gentle rocking motion of the cart and soft sounds of bells on jesses.

↞ ↠

The Nobles relaxed in the shade of a large pine tree as their camp was erected around them. Dogs ran between the tents and hung around the campfires, waiting for scraps. The falconers busied themselves, staking out the birds on perches in the middle of the camp. The three first-years were placed on the day watch to protect the birds from predators.

When dusk approached, the birds were again placed in the Mews Cart to protect them from owls.

The noble's rowdiness increased as the sky reddened with the setting sun. Charlie lay beside his friends in their bedrolls under the Mews Cart, trying to fall asleep. He groaned and rolled onto his side. He opened his eyes and found Wesley staring at him.

"I never knew they got drunk on these trips," Wesley said quietly.

Charlie looked at him, puzzled, "I guess I just never thought about it. It makes sense in a way. No one's wife came with them. I just hope they can sit in their saddles tomorrow," he chuckled.

Wesley smirked. "Seeing The King topple off his horse would be funny."

Charlie's eyes went wide, "Shhhh, don't let anyone hear you make fun of The King."

46

Wesley's face dropped. He forgot who he was pretending to be and the station he was currently in, "Oh, you're right. I apologize; please don't tell anyone."

"Don't worry, my friend. It would be hard not to laugh at it, though." Charlie grinned and rolled back over.

Wesley swallowed the lump in his throat and cringed at his misspeak. As he got closer to these boys, he could tell it would be harder and harder to keep the secret. Charlie and Alex were so easy to talk to, always telling stories of their past and asking about his. Making up stories that were loosely based on the truth was hard, to say the least. Hopefully, he could remember all his lies.

The sun rose too soon the next day. The falconers and dog handlers were up with it, preparing for the morning's hunt. The Nobles, however, were still snoring loudly, ensuring no quarry would be near them.

Master Kenton walked over to the pantry wagon and waved to Alex. Alex's face brightened and ran over to him.

"Yes, Sir?" Alex asked.

"Can you reach inside there and grab that very back pot? But be very careful. Do not knock any other pans over; everyone is still sleeping."

"Yes, Sir," he said confidently. Alex climbed up on the wagon's side and leaned in as far as he could. "What a silly place to store a pot." He mumbled under his breath. His feet slipped slightly on the wheel, and he tittered a little.

"Sorry, son," Master Kenton said quietly.

"What was that, Sir…" He started to say right before someone pushed his foot off the wheel. Alex's hands went out to the side, trying to keep himself from face-planting in the wagon to no avail. His hands found nothing to stop his forward progress. With a mighty crash of pots, pans, and other staples, his whole body disappeared into the wagon.

"Stay hidden now," Master Kenton whispered.

Shouts and commotion could be heard inside the Nobles' tents.

"What is that god-awful racket out there?" The King bellowed.

An attendant ran out of the tent to investigate.

"What happened? Is everything okay out here?" He asked in a rush.

"Just fine, Jessup. Everyone is fine. Can you please inform The King that everything is ready for him when he desires?" Master Kenton said with a calm expression as if nothing happened.

Jessup walked over to the pantry wagon and peered inside. Alex glanced up at him and smiled shyly. "I see." Is all he said as he walked back to The King's tent.

"Hurry! Get out of there," Kenton said to Alex. Alex eagerly complied.

"What was all that about?" He dared ask.

"Sometimes Nobles need a push out of bed, so to speak," he said with a smile.

↞ → ↠

Soon, the entire camp was active, and the hunt was underway.

Everyone walked through the field as if choreographed: dogs and their handlers going first, bird-less falconers, apprentices, and attendants, each holding a long stick going next, followed closely by the mounted Nobles and Master Kenton, each with a bird on their fists.

After a few moments of flushing, they were rewarded with a bouquet of pheasants taking wing. The King released

48

his silver Gyrfalcon. As was proper, his bird always took the day's first flight.

His falcon picked out one of the pheasants and took chase. She sliced through the sky with deadly precision, banking one way and then the next, tracking behind its unlucky prey. The pheasant never stood a chance, and the chase was over in short order. Several falconers rushed forward to retrieve The King's bird.

The rest of the morning was conducted in the same manner. One bird at a time was released until The King tired and returned to camp.

⇇ ⇉

"Boys, gather round," Master Kenton said.

The three apprentices jumped to attention.

"You have been taught that we keep the birds always wanting more, correct?" He asked them.

"Yes, Sir." They replied as one.

"And why is that? Wesley?"

"Um, well, um… a hungry bird will listen, and a full one will not," he stammered.

"That is very true. However, a bird that is always hungry might not be responsive forever. You have to reward excellent behavior. Those birds that caught quarry today will be fed up. They will be useless for a few days, but they will be happy. So, what is the lesson you have learned? Charlie?"

"Keep them wanting until they do what you desire and then feed them until they are content but not fully satisfied."

"Very good. Get some rest; it's the same thing tomorrow."

Five days later, The King finally tired of hunting and returned to the Castle.

Chapter 7

The year finally came to a close for the apprentices. Charlie and Alex walked Wesley to the stable.

"Hope you have a good trip back home," Alex said.

"Thanks. It's only a couple of days' ride back," he replied, keeping his eyes on the ground.

"Have a great summer break; see you at harvest time." Charlie beamed. "Hey, maybe you'll see Prince William returning from the University. That would be a sight."

Wesley frowned, "Why is that?"

"Oh, I don't know. I have always envied him in a way. Seeing him up close would just be great."

"I've never seen him up close, have you?" Wesley asked, still avoiding eye contact.

Charlie shook his head, "No, only from the balcony in the square. I probably wouldn't even recognize him if he didn't have all of his attendants around him."

Wesley laughed despite himself, "You know? I think you're right."

They said the rest of their goodbyes and parted ways, each heading to his own home.

Wesley walked his rented mare until he could no longer see the other two boys. After he was sure they would not see him, he headed back toward the Castle. He entered the delivery gate and tied his mare to a hitching post. He entered the kitchen and took the same path to his room. He did what seemed like a lifetime ago.

Once back in his room, adequately bathed and clothed, he once again went to find his mother and father.

"William, my boy." His mother squealed when she saw him walking through the hall.

"Mother, I'm so happy to see you."

"Oh, my boy, look how you've grown. But look at your hands and face! Why have you spent so much time outside? They weren't making you work, were they? And what did you do to your hair? It's so short, I almost didn't recognize you."

He blushed fiercely and raised a hand to his cheek. "Oh, um… they have wonderful study alcoves in an open-air court. I spent much of my free time there, that is all, nothing more. And I thought I needed a change with my hair," he said, thinking quickly.

"Well, I suppose it suits you since you are still young, but be more careful next year." She grabbed his arm and led him to the Throne Room. "And my, how strong you are now. Your bride-to-be will be very impressed with that."

He smiled at his mother and nodded his head.

Chapter 8

"Wesley! Over here!" William turned in a circle to locate the voice. He saw Charlie sitting beside another boy near the fountain in the town square.

"Welcome back. How was your summer?" Charlie asked him.

"Good, and yours?"

"Couldn't have been better. I slept in late every day and did much of nothing all day long. Wesley, this is my best friend, Chadwick. Chadwick, this is Wesley."

Chadwick held out his hand, "Glad to know you. This guy says great things about you."

"Really?"

"Truly." Chadwick nodded his head.

"So, have you decided what to try for this year?" Charlie asked his friend.

"Smithing," Chadwick said with a sly smile.

"Smithing? You've got to be joking. You hate smithing."

Chadwick dropped his eyes, "It's not as bad as I made it out to be. Quite a noble profession, you know."

"I know that. I always assumed you would follow in your father's footsteps," Charlie teased.

"You did?" Chadwick exclaimed with surprise.

"Of course. I knew you only chose falconry because of me. I'm happy for you."

"Well, I haven't made it yet. I still must be chosen."

"Have you made it back to see your girl?"

"My girl?" Chadwick asked, clearly confused.

"Mariann?"

Chadwick blushed fiercely, "Oh, her! Um, yes, but only a couple of times."

"You went back to the Burrows?"

Chadwick shook his head adamantly, "No, she found me first, and then we started meeting near the border."

"She must like you."

He nodded, "I think so, but I also think she is very jealous. Her expression clouds when we start to talk about how our lives are different, so I try not to bring it up."

"Is her bother here, or does he already have an apprenticeship?"

"That's another different thing. They don't participate in Choosing Day."

"By choice?"

Chadwick shook his head, "They've never even heard of it."

"I'm sure they are just saying that. How can you not know about Choosing Day?"

"I don't think so, Charlie. Her brother, Fredrick, came with me today. He's sixteen and not yet an apprentice. The guards stopped him, Charlie. They asked who his father was and where they lived. They wouldn't let him in."

"That doesn't make sense."

"No, it doesn't. What is going on, Charlie? How can two groups of people in one city be treated so differently?"

Charlie slapped him on the back, "I don't have any answers, but you need to focus on your future right now. You will do just fine this year. I'll see you later. We have to go check in."

"What was all that about?" Wesley asked as they walked to The House.

Charlie told him about his last conversation with Chadwick. Wesley frowned but did not reply or comment.

"Welcome back, second-years." Trevor once again met them in front of The House. "This year will be different. More challenging, more work, but more rewarding. Here are your room assignments. You have the same roommate but new rooms." He handed each pair an envelope. "You will find your first quarters schedules inside, dismissed."

The boys departed. "Well, that was easier this year. See you in the kitchen?" Alex asked his friends.

"You know it. See you soon."

Charlie and Wesley were assigned to the dogs for the first quarter. But this time, instead of cleaning up after them, they were learning how to train them. Wesley had a knack for it; Charlie struggled to get the dogs to respect him.

"You just have to hold yourself in a manner that says I am in control over you, not the other way around," Wesley told him one day halfway through the quarter.

"I don't know if I can do that. Dogs and I are just too friendly to each other for that. I think I will do better with the birds."

"Well, let's hope so," Wesley teased.

Their next quarter assignment was in the mews. They were learning to handle the more experienced birds. Charlie was right; he was better at handling the birds, but to Wesley's delight, he also excelled.

"Are you ready for your first free flight, men?" David asked them.

"Yes, Sir," the four said together.

"Good, go grab your bird and meet me outside." They hurried into the mews and retrieved their assigned bird.

They pretended the birds were fresh captures and handled them as such even though they were past their hunting age. Most birds would be used for several years and then released back into the wild. A select few truly tame birds were retained each year to train the new falconers.

Out in the practice yard, an audience had appeared. A small group of young Nobles was in the stands watching. Wesley froze in the doorway.

"Don't tell me you've got stage fright?" Thaddeus scoffed.

"Of, of course not." Wesley proceeded, keeping his chin low and eyes on his bird. He knew several of those boys; if they cared to look, they would surely recognize him.

After their lesson, Wesley hurried off the field and back into the privacy of the mews and away from prying eyes. Once alone, he let out a sigh of relief.

He was the first to put away his bird; all he wanted was to get back to his room and close the door tightly. He rushed out of the mews and rounded a corner straight into one of the young Nobles.

"Slow down there, you fool," he yelled, picking himself off the floor.

"I'm sorry, sir. Please forgive me, excuse me." Wesley tried to rush past him. The noble grabbed his arm and spun him around.

"William!! Is that you?" He asked in complete shock. The noble looked him up and down and then realized that he was gripping the arm of the Crown Prince. He dropped his hands and did a hasty bow. "My apologies, Your Highness." He added quickly. "What are you doing here, looking like this?"

"Something my father insisted on, please don't say anything to anyone, Gregory. You are sworn to silence, do you hear?" William said with a hushed voice.

Gregory stood a little taller, "Sworn to silence by a falconer? Where's your ring for me to kiss? You know that is the only way that binding works."

"Gregory, please. I'll find you later and explain everything. Just do me a favor and tell no one. Those are orders from The King." William glared at his once friend.

Gregory smirked and then chuckled, "Of course, my friend, your secret is safe with me."

William sighed with relief, "I'll find you tonight. Come to the kitchen for a late-night snack." Gregory nodded. William glanced around but, seeing no one, hurried back to his room.

Charlie stood just around the corner, out of sight from Wesley and the Noble, hearing all that was said. Wesley was Prince William? Why hadn't he noticed the resemblance before? Should he tell him that he knows or pretend to know nothing? *I must say something; I can't hide things very well,* he thought.

He hesitated for a moment in front of the door to their room. He steeled himself and then walked in. Wesley was lying on his bed face first. Charlie walked over to his bed and sat down.

"Want to talk about it?" He asked him.

Wesley turned his face, "About what?"

"About your conversation with the Noble back there. I, um, I overheard you. I didn't mean to eavesdrop. I didn't see you at first. I saw a Noble and thought I would wait for him to leave. Um, are you okay?"

Wesley's face was ash white. He slowly sat up and swung his legs around. "So, um, you heard *everything*?" Charlie nodded. "Well, I'm not sure what to say. Um." He paused, scratching his head.

Charlie held out his hand, "Hi, I'm Charlie," he said.

Wesley looked at his hand and then up at his face; he didn't appear to be mocking him. "Hi Charlie, I'm William, but please call me Wesley," he said slowly, shaking his hand.

"Nice to meet Wesley. So, what brings you to The House?"

Wesley sighed and told him the whole story, how his father wanted him to learn how to connect to everyday people and learn how to be a falconer.

After he was finished, Charlie reflected for a moment. "Why would he have you become a falconer and not a knight or something?"

"I asked him that same question. He said falconry would do. He is so hard to talk to."

"I think all fathers are like that," Charlie laughed.

Wesley looked at Charlie and laughed with him.

←→

Charlie and Wesley spent more time with just the two of them for the remainder of the year. Alex still joined them occasionally, but their schedules were different. Wesley told Charlie new stories of his childhood, the true tales of the ones he spun before.

When summer break came again, they parted ways, but this time, they both knew the truth about where they would be spending the summer.

Chapter 9

Halfway through their third year, they were finally permitted to go on a hunt as a handler. It was a lesser hunt but an excellent first experience for them.

"The Count and Countess of Thornburg are visiting The King to finalize the marriage of their daughter to the Crown Prince. The King has offered them a chance to hunt with the Royal birds in the morning," Master Kenton said, "I am taking the third- and fourth-years with me."

Cheers erupted from those going, and then everyone set into motion to prepare for the hunt.

↞ ↠

Charlie and Wesley sat in front of a small fire that evening, staring at the stars and stealing glances at the Count of Thornburg's daughter and her attendants. It was unusual for a daughter to attend a hunt, wives on occasion, yes, and most definitely sons, but rarely a daughter.

"She's pretty. Have you spent any time with her?" Charlie whispered.

Wesley shook his head, "We met once when I was eleven. That is when my father set up the marriage. I haven't seen her since. She is quite fetching."

"Quite fetching?" Charlie laughed. "Spoken like a true prince, not a commoner."

Wesley's cheeks reddened, "Sorry, she is very pretty." Then he started to laugh.

Emily and her attendant glanced their way, whispering to each other.

"When's the wedding?"

Wesley swallowed loudly, "Not sure. I guess my father will be decided that soon."

"Do you think he will get word to you soon or wait until summer break?"

"Oh, he'll wait till summer. That is just the thing he would do."

Before they knew it, summer break was upon them. Goodbyes were short as everyone was welcoming the break. Wesley sat on his bed, the last to leave. For the past couple of weeks, he had been growing more and more agitated. Charlie was the only one who knew why. He would be finding out when his wedding was to take place. Would his father call for him, or should he confront him? The latter might make his father think he was eager; the former might make him think he was avoiding him. Neither was ideal.

He decided to change into the clothes he brought with him. The last time he snuck into his room, he was almost caught.

He walked through the deserted halls of The House and then the short walk through the grounds to the Castle. When he showed them his ring, the guards at the main doors snapped to attention. He grinned and shook his head. Once he was a little older and allowed to reside in the Castle full-time again, they would recognize him when he approached.

He walked through the halls of the Castle, servants, and attendants scurrying quickly one way or another.

"Prince William, your back!" Edward called from down the hall.

"How have you been, Edward?" He responded as he approached.

"Dreadfully bored, Sir. I still do not know why I cannot attend to you at The University?"

"Students are not allowed to have servants. I must learn to do for myself."

Edward scoffed at this, "The Crown Prince, future King of Weshingham, *does not* have to learn *to do* for himself," he said sternly, waggling his finger at him.

"Well, the Crown Prince doesn't have to tolerate a finger waggle either." Edward dropped his hand, and William laughed heartily, slapping his attendant on the shoulder, "Come, let's find my mother."

"No time for that. Your father wishes to see you as soon as you arrive."

"Well, at least I didn't have to wait long," he grumbled.

⟵ ⟶

"Prince William!" The herald called out as William walked into the Throne Room. The counselors stood and bowed as he walked to the throne.

"Welcome home, son," King Robert said, gesturing to his mother's throne, inviting him to sit.

"Glad to be home, my King," William said formally.

"How have your studies been going?" His father asked him quietly.

"Surprisingly rewarding, but I have some questions when you have a moment," he replied. His father smiled at him and patted his shoulder.

William sat on his mother's throne, listening to his father's counselors arguing about one thing and then another. He knew he should be paying more attention to what they were saying, but he had plenty of time to learn the workings of the court. A few hours later, the King called the meeting over and retired to his waiting room with William.

"So, my boy. You now have a choice to make."

"Father?"

"Marry this harvest… or finish your fourth year."

"You are allowing me this choice?"

"You are almost 18 years old, almost a man. You will be running this kingdom someday. It is time for you to start making choices for yourself. If you are old enough to marry and start your own family, then you must be allowed to choose when it happens." William didn't know what to say. "Rat got your tongue?"

"I'm sorry. You caught me off guard. It is just so unexpected. I was expecting to come in here today and be told everything about my wedding was already settled, the date set, dress commissioned, and cake in the oven."

Robert tilted his head back and let loose a loud bellow of a laugh. "So, what is this question you have?"

William hung his head and raked his hands through his sandy blonde hair. Slowly, he repeated what he had heard about the Burrows and some boys not being allowed into the Choosing Day.

"All the answers you seek will be revealed to you soon. Come, my boy. Your mother is eager to see you, too. Think about your future and tell me at dinner tonight."

Chapter 10

Wesley arrived early and was waiting in their shared room when Charlie arrived.

"Wesley, I was beginning to think you weren't coming back this year."

"I was given the choice."

"And you chose this over being a prince. I think the smell of this place is getting to you," Charlie laughed.

"I've never been given a choice before, and the thought of not finishing something I started didn't sit well with me."

"And what about the wedding? I haven't heard any announcements yet."

"I was given a choice about that as well. It will be set for next harvest."

"Another year as a bachelor. That's great," Charlie teased.

⟵⟶

"Isn't she beautiful?" Wesley asked, looking at his new bird as she stood on her perch, staring at him with total fright in her eyes.

"She is a beautiful Peregrine. I bet she will quickly become the Queens' favorite," Charlie told him.

"I'm going to call her Liz."

"What do you think about mine, though, mighty striking as well?" Charlie asked, admiring his Silver Gyrfalcon.

It was only by sheer luck that he got this bird. The trappers arrived a week ago with six crates. It was highly unusual for all the trapping teams to come back at the same time. Master Kenton placed the crates in a line, not knowing what kind of bird they contained. He then randomly drew the six fourth-year apprentices' names from a bowl. Wesley, Lance, and Malick each chose a crate with a Peregrine falcon. Thaddeus received a Merlin, and Alex received a Prairie. Charlie went last and was rewarded with the best bird of all. Typically, the Gyrfalcon was trained only by the Master Falconer, but Master Kenton was already training two captured a few weeks earlier.

"It is an honor to be training that bird, that is for sure," Wesley told him.

"You don't have to tell me that. I haven't been able to sleep a wink since getting her."

"Better not lose her on her first free flight," he joked.

"Oh, she is never free-flying," Charlie joked back.

← →

The training process was slow at first. When the trappers first obtained the birds, they placed their training jesses on them - large, sturdy leather strips with metal swivels. A long leash was then attached to that. When the birds arrived at the Mews, they were scared beyond belief and huddled in the corner of their crate.

The first step was to get the birds to sit on the falconer's fist and their perches. At first, the bird would just fall over, refusing to grip anything. After a few tries, the birds would finally grip the falconer's gloved fist but then try to fly away. They would lunge and come to the end of the shortened leash. Some would flap for a few moments before eventually hanging from the glove by their jesses. The falconer would gently spin them around with their hand against their back and tilt them back onto the glove. Some birds learned the lesson quicker than others. Charlie's bird was one of the few that refused to learn that it couldn't get away.

The next step came after the bird would sit peacefully on the fist. Walking around. Most of the birds would immediately bait off the glove at the slightest movement.

Getting the birds to take meat from the falconer was also important. After a few days, however, all the birds accepted tidbits of meat with little hesitation. Hunger was a powerful training tool, and for the new birds, the only food they received was given by hand. They needed to learn that the only way to obtain food was from the falconer. The falconer was now its master.

"Hey, Charlie!" Wesley called.

"How's it going with Liz?" Charlie asked, walking over to him. Sky sat calmly on Charlie's fist.

"Not good. She just won't take enough quail from me. She feels lighter. I think she is losing weight. I'm worried. If she doesn't start eating well by tomorrow night, Master Kenton says we will have to release her, and even then, she might die."

"Wow, that's extreme. I'm sure she will come around. Being dependent on someone is new to her. She will learn that this is the best way, the easiest way. She is past her first molt. I know the trappers like haggards, because they already know how to hunt successfully, but older birds are harder to tame. Get them young, and they mold easily."

"We learned that, yes," he nodded, "but I didn't realize how true it was."

By the end of the week, all the birds would sit on the fist without baiting while the falconers walked around the training yard and eagerly took any meat offered, including Liz.

Over the next few weeks, each falconer worked with their bird, getting them used to whistle commands. Teaching them to hop from a perch to the fist and eventually making short flights to the fist with a long leash, called a creance, attached.

Before the birds could hunt free again, they would have to learn to listen to the falconer during distraction and learn to fly dependably without a leash.

The day was calm, and the sky was bright. The training area was bustling with activity, and the stands were packed with Nobles and commoners alike.

Charlie whistled and then held his breath as Sky took wing and sailed across the King's courtyard, performing her first truly free flight with flawless precision. No nets above to keep an unruly bird in check. Charlie rewarded her flight with a tidbit of food as he reattached her lead.

"Great job, Falconer Charlie," Master Kenton said loudly. The King and Queen clapped as Charlie was given the royal blue tunic of a Falconer. He did it; he made it.

Wesley was up next; he looked even more nervous than Charlie felt.

He walked to the perch in the middle of the court and placed Liz on it. After removing her leash, he walked across the court, held up his fist, and whistled. Liz looked up, shook herself once, and then took flight. She sailed swiftly and gracefully across the courtyard. She swooped down low, her wingtips almost brushing across the grass. As she neared Wesley, she soared almost straight up and latched onto his fist to snatch the tidbit held between his gloved fingers.

Wesley smiled broadly, looking up at The King and Queen for the first time.

The King stood clapping, the Queen's eyes went wide, and a hand flew to her mouth as she looked at the man down below, recognition dawning on her.

"Congratulations, Falconer Wesley," Master Kenton said loudly.

↞ ↠

After the ceremony, Charlie, Wesley, Alex, and the others treated themselves to a visit to a pub not far from The House.

Charlie stood and cleared his throat loudly, "I just wanted to say that these last four years have been the happiest of my life. A massive blur that seemed to last forever and leave far too quickly all at the same time."

"Here, here!" Everyone shouted and took a drink.

Charlie sat and spoke quietly to Wesley. "How much time do you have left? When must you return?"

"Tomorrow, I'm afraid. I'm nervous, though."

Charlie stared at him, "How so?"

"I think my mother recognized me today. She was led to believe that I had been at the university the whole time. I'm not sure how she will take this."

"Won't your father explain?"

He raked his hands through his hair, "I hope so. My father told me to write to her, and I had to invent things to tell her. I tried to be vague, but it was still a lie."

"Don't worry about it. I have a feeling everything will work out fine."

"I hope you're right."

↞ ↠

Charlie paused at the bulletin board in the kitchen. The Harvest Festival was going to be in 3 weeks. He was looking forward to it this year. On the first day of the festival, the falconers were allowed to take their pick of most of the birds and go hunting without the Nobles. It was the highlight of the year for a falconer.

He glanced over the other notices, seeing nothing of interest until his eyes passed over a Royal Wedding Announcement. *So, it was finally going to happen.*

Prince William and Lady Emily would be married on the last day of the Harvest Festival. Charlie grinned. He hoped his friend would be happy.

"I see you heard the news," a voice said from behind him. Charlie turned around to find William standing there, wearing his falconry tunic.

"Good to see you again, Wesley," Charlie said with a smile, "What brings you back here?"

"Looking for a little bird time with a friend, I guess," he said with a shrug. "I miss Liz, how's she doing?"

"I took her out yesterday; she's just as graceful as ever. Come on, I was on my way to the Mews now."

They walked in companionable silence to the mews. When they arrived, they were the only ones there.

"Everything go all right with your mom?"

"Yeah, my father explained everything before I saw her again. She was just happy that I was home to stay, regardless of where I had been. Royal decree and all, there really wasn't anything she could do about it," William chuckled.

Charlie nodded, "So, are you excited about the wedding?"

"Extremely, I have gotten to know Emily over the past few months. She is a wonderful person. I wish I could invite you to the wedding and introduce you to her. It is strange, I finally made a true friend, but I can't be seen with you. I don't like it at all."

"It's ok. We get to see each other while hunting, and you can visit the Mews any time you want. I can even give the prince a personal tour sometime," he said with a wink.

William smiled, "You know what, I think I'm going to take you up on that. I'll bring Emily along with me." He nodded. "I have a surprise for you. My father told me what his wedding present to me would be. He is allowing me to pick any bird to have as my own, including the Silver Gyr."

"Truly? That's an amazing gift."

"I always thought I would have to wait until I became King to get a Gyrfalcon."

"Well, let me show you the ones we are training."

William shook his head. "I have already chosen my first bird. I would like Sky to be my first with you as her handler."

"I am honored, Your Highness." Charlie bowed.

"Stop that." William punched him in the arm.

"Sorry, I'm just practicing."

"Very funny. Now, let's exercise a couple of birds."

Chapter 11

On the last day of the Harvest Festival, the entire Kingdom was in full celebration mode. Flowers were placed on every street corner throughout the city to honor the prince and his bride-to-be.

The Royal Wedding took place early in the morning. The reception started right after and continued well into the evening hours. The entire Castle was lit up with the soft glow of the electric lights. At midnight, the Castles' lights were turned off as one, and then the entire sky erupted in bright lights as the best fireworks display ever shown took flight with whistles and loud explosions.

The day after was declared a Holiday of Rest and all businesses were closed.

Charlie walked through the deserted streets of the Market, marveling that everyone agreed to close up shop and stay home. Walking the streets with nothing but the occasional stray dog or scurrying mouse as company was strange.

He stopped at the center fountain and took the opposite road instead of returning to the castle like usual. The Burrows were separated from the rest of the city by a small creek that wound lazily through the city. The bridge over the creek was wide enough for two carriages to pass each other easily. Waterfowl lined the creek on both sides, quacking to one another noisily.

The other side of the creek looked no different at first. Large multi-family homes lined the streets on both sides, with a few warehouses and businesses in between. Slowly, dwellings disappeared and were replaced with the trade district. Most of the guilds had their headquarters in the heart of the district. Charlie and Chadwick had been to the district occasionally with Chadwick's father.

Charlie walked past the closed businesses and guild houses. The further he walked, the less familiar the city looked. The homes and other buildings looked more run down; there were fewer flowers and trees, and there were many more people. No one here seemed to be celebrating the Royal Wedding. Charlie looked at the people he passed. They were just as Chadwick described, thin and depressed looking.

He turned a corner and saw a large circular courtyard with a large fountain in the middle. The fountain had a statue of a majestic Gyrfalcon with its wings stretched out. The Gyrfalcon's head was pointed up, and a strong stream of water flowed from its beak. It would have been an impressive-looking fountain if it had been maintained. Moss grew around the fountain's base, and vines wound their way up the legs and wings of the falcon. The water itself didn't look much better, being tinged slightly green.

Next to the fountain was a royal supply wagon handing out bread to everyone assembled. Charlie grinned and walked over to one of the guards, trying to keep everyone in an orderly line.

"Get in line if you want anything," the guard said gruffly.

"I'm fine, Sir. Just out for a walk."

"Move on. No loitering during the Giving."

"I'm sorry, Sir. I am a falconer, so I am unfamiliar with The Burrows. I thought the Giving had been suspended?"

The guard sighed and looked Charlie up and down before answering. "When the people do not follow the law, their Giving is withheld. These people here have been good citizens lately.”

Charlie frowned.

“Is there a problem?”

“I’m not sure. I’m just confused. We don’t have the Giving or threat of not having it on the other side of the city.”

“Keep your voice down, or I will be forced to arrest you for inciting a riot.”

Charlie held up his hands in surrender. “Oh, no. I’m sorry, this is just all new to me.”

“You better head back to your part of the city and stay there for your own safety.”

“Yes, Sir. Thank you.”

Whatever this Giving was, Charlie didn’t like the sound of it. It sounded like the King withheld the Giving from these citizens until they pleased him. It rubbed him the wrong way but sounded eerily familiar simultaneously.

He soon found himself back at The House. He started to walk back to his private room but didn’t feel like being closed up inside all day. He continued to the Mews - his favorite place to spend his free time.

The winter months passed, and then spring was in full bloom. The Mews was in full motion, preparing for the upcoming Royal hunt. The birds still saw plenty of action in the winter months, but only with Lesser Lords and their families. Their hunts were more laid back with less fanfare.

With the first Royal Hunt of the year, everything was polished; new equipment was made, new gloves commissioned, new jesses and shiny new bells for every bird, and hoods were re-plumed. This was also going to be the first hunt for Princess Emily. Master Kenton picked out a beautiful Prairie falcon for her.

↞ ↠

Prince William and Princess Emily strolled through the camp, admiring the birds staked out on their perches. They spoke quietly, holding hands as they went. Charlie saw them and smiled. William honestly looked happy, and if Charlie wasn't imagining it, the Princess looked like she was expecting.

Later that evening, after the moon was high and the stars twinkled brightly, Prince William asked Charlie if he could see his Gyrfalcon, Sky.

"Is she ready for her first Royal hunt?" William asked.

"Most definitely. She is ready and willing."

"Good. Father is allowing me the honor of the first flight tomorrow."

Charlie's mouth dropped, "Great honor indeed."

"I hope she flies true and quick."

"She will, you'll see. If I may be so bold?"

"Yes, anything."

"Will the family be growing soon?"

William smiled, "Noticeable, is it?"

Charlie nodded, "Only slightly. It could have been the gown's cut, but I didn't think it was."

"Twins, we are told."

"Congratulations."

↞ ↠

True to Charlie's word, Sky performed flawlessly the following morning. The first partridge they found she took off immediately from Prince Williams' fist and knocked it from the sky with a poof of feathers. The partridge

72

plummeted to the ground. Sky twisted in the air, dove down, and snapped the neck in one quick motion. Charlie rushed over, removed her from her catch, and rewarded her. She happily forgot about the partridge for the plump quail on his fist.

The King retired early from the hunt and let the younger party members continue without him.

Overall, the hunt went well, and everyone returned to camp happy and satisfied.

With the coming of summer came the molting season for the birds. Feathers were shed, and new feathers were grown. In the wild, these birds were susceptible to predators and starvation, but under the care of falconers, they were well-fed and cared for during this trying time.

This summer also brought with it the birth of twin princes. Prince Robert and Prince Wesley were welcomed to the Kingdom with a week of celebrations.

As soon as Charlie heard about the birth of the princes, he rushed off to a toymaker, bought two plush kestrel toys, and had them sent to the Castle.

Prince William brought Princess Emily and the boys to the Mews three days after the Royal Celebration.

Charlie was surprised to see the Royal Family walking around so soon but delighted to see his friend.

"Greetings, Your Highness." Charlie bowed.

Emily smiled, but William frowned. He hated Charlie calling him that.

Charlie gave him a knowing wink. "Would you like to see the birds today? They aren't looking their best right now, but they're happy." He led them through the Mews, answering Emily's questions; she knew little about the birds.

"Are you the one that sent the toys?" She asked near the end of the tour.

"Yes, ma'am. I hope you like them," he replied.

"It was a welcomed surprise," she responded. "William, I think the boys and I will retire. I thought I was up to this, but I feel that I am fading."

"Of course, Em." He gestured for an attendant to come forward and handed him the basket with both boys in it. "I am going to stay behind a few moments longer." He kissed her on the cheek before she departed.

"Fine boys, you have," Charlie said.

"Thanks. Are there any girls in your life right now?"

Charlie shook his head, "I don't have time to even look. I spend all my time with the birds."

"Well, my friend, you must get out and live beyond these walls," William said as they ambled through the Mews.

"I'll think about it. I did take a walk through the city after your wedding."

"That was some time ago."

Charlie rubbed the back of his neck. "That is was."

"Where did you go?"

"The Burrows."

"The Burrows? Strange place for a stroll."

"I won't be returning, that is for sure. Have you ever heard of the Gracious Reward?" Charlie asked with slight hesitation.

William stopped and looked at Charlie, "No."

"Well, I'm not sure what it is either. I just thought you might," Charlie fumbled. If William didn't know about it, then he probably shouldn't be talking about it.

"I'll have to ask my father."

Suddenly, the relative quiet of the Mews was shattered by a series of bells. William's face went ashen.

"What's wrong? What do those bells mean?" Charlie looked around franticly. Were they under attack?

"There's something wrong with the King. Please come with me."

"Me, whoa, wait. You want me to go with you?" Charlie stammered.

"My father's health has been declining. He hasn't said anything, but I can see it in my mother's eyes. I don't want to see him alone. Please." William looked at Charlie, waiting for his answer.

"Okay. I'll go."

They rushed through the Castle. Charlie tried to keep up while still looking around. He was entering parts of the Castle he had never been to before and most likely never would again.

Two guards outside the King's private room crossed their lances across the door.

William glared at them.

"You may enter, your Highness, but not him."

"He is with me. We will both enter. Now stand aside," he said with a commanding voice. Charlie glanced at his friend. He sounded so much more confident than he had ever heard him. This was Prince William, not Falconer Wesley, standing beside him.

The guards relented and opened the door. The Queen was next to the King's bed. She smiled when she saw William and held out a hand to him. He rushed to her side.

"How is he?" He whispered. She shook her head but said nothing. William looked down at his father. His face was a white sheet, and he looked sickly.

Charlie stayed near the door, giving the Royals privacy.

The King opened his eyes and settled them on William.

"Ah, William, my boy. I'm afraid you will be King sooner than I planned."

"Come now, Father, it is not that bad."

He shook his head ever so slightly, "No…I am not fit to rule, even if I live through the night." The Queen started to sob. King Robert held up a hand. She grabbed it quickly and brought it to her lips. "You will be named King at once."

"Father…" He paused, not knowing how to put his thoughts into words.

"Yes, my son?"

"You, um, you never taught me how to rule," he said softly and quickly added. "I have sat in on council meetings with you and petitions with Mother, but you have failed to teach me how to govern." He kept his eyes on his father's chest, refusing to look him in the eye. His father's chest rose and fell with labored breathing.

"Oh, my son, but I have." William frowned, "Your schooling has prepared you well."

"My schooling was falconry. Not governing," he said, shocked and confused.

"My dear boy. People and birds are the same. Treat the people as you would a falcon, and they will love you. You have learned to keep the falcons wanting more to gain their attention and acceptance. Governing people is much the same. If you give the populous just enough, keep them looking to you as their protector; they will love you." Suddenly, his face contorted as several deep, raspy coughs shook his body.

"Answer me this then. What is the Gracious Reward?"

The King's eyes locked on his sons. "When the people do as they should, I am gracious. That is why I am loved."

"Then why have I never heard of it before?"

"The poorer communities in the kingdom are riddled with crime and disobedience; they need… extra incentives." He paused again to steady his breathing, "As I said," he continued after a few moments. "You were given the best schooling I could offer you, your Majesty. To train a falcon… to govern a people." King Robert closed his eyes to rest.

William glanced over to Charlie. Charlie nodded and bowed low to the new King, thinking to himself, *To train a falcon, to govern a people? The Gracious Reward is training the people.*

Chapter 12

William was to be crowned a few weeks later in grand style. Royals from all the surrounding kingdoms were invited to the celebration.

The day before his coronation, foreign kings, queens, dukes, princes, and princesses started to arrive. The Castle staff was in full swing, scurrying through the corridors, making sure all the guest suites were pristine and ready for their Royal company.

Not since the day King Robert had been coronated had the Castle and the Kingdom seen so many Royals in one place.

The citizens lined the streets all day, watching the procession of armed guards on horseback and royal carriages as they rolled past. Brightly colored carriages trimmed in gold and silver pulled by proud, spirited horses. The liverymen sat poised with straight backs and stoic expressions as they passed the throng of people clamoring for a peek at a carriage occupant. Falconers on foot and horseback trailed after the carriages carrying a variety of falcons and other birds.

Master Kenton and his falconers waited at the castle's main gates to escort the falconers to the mews and their quarters.

The foreign guards entered the courtyard and circled the immense space before the carriages rolled in. The horses' hooves on the cobblestone and the squeaking and groaning of the carriages created a cacophony of sound.

The falconers entered last carrying their birds on their fists.

Charlie glanced around, looking for a mews cart, but didn't see any. Were they the only Kingdom that used them? He found that strange.

He looked at each of the birds as they were brought in. Most he recognized, but a few of them, he had no idea what kind they were. Some were small, the size of a Kestrel or a Merlin, but some were so large that the falconer had a staff to support their arm as they walked.

Master Kenton led the procession to the mews yard. While the mews could hold 30 birds, they had no vacant perches at the moment. Numerous perches had been arranged around the training yard. The new falconers walked through the perches, picking which one they wanted for their charges. When all the birds were staked out and fed, Master Kenton led the falconers to The House and showed them their quarters.

←→

Early the following day, after Charlie checked on the King's birds, he strolled through the training yard marveling at the vast array of birds staked out.

He stopped before a striking bluish-grey bird with dark barring across its slightly grey breast. It had a long tail, short legs, and thick toes above its long talons. The bird spread its wings out as it stretched and flapped them slightly. Charlie stared at the long yet broad wings with rounded tips.

"Beautiful, isn't she?" A voice said from behind him. He turned to see a young man not much older than him standing with his arms crossed.

"What kind is she?" Charlie asked.

"An Accipiter, more commonly called a Goshawk."

"An accipiter? They are untrainable! Why do you have it here? She looks so calm." Charlie said in surprise.

"Oh, they are quite trainable if you know how. Just like falcons, but different quarry."

"Is that a Golden Eagle?" Charlie gasped, looking at the enormous bird tethered further away from all the other birds. It looked over at Charlie, appearing to size him up.

"Yes, King Roogan likes them. He likes to strike fear in those around him, and a giant bird like that does the job nicely. Not to mention his hell hounds," the falconer told him.

"Hell hound? What is that?" Charlie's eyes widen.

"Oh, nothing as terrible as it sounds, really. Just a large breed of dog he has developed. Most of them are very friendly, but their howl is terrifying. My name is Rus." He held his hand out.

Charlie grasped it, "I'm Charlie."

"I would love to see your birds."

"Then, by all means, follow me." Charlie smiled broadly.

Chapter 13

"Are you ready?" Queen Izabella asked William. He stood before a large mirror while an attendant affixed his cape on his shoulders.

"I think so," he said and then sighed loudly.

Queen Izabella motioned for the attendant to leave. He quickly bowed and departed.

"What's the matter?" She asked her son.

He sat down on a stool near the mirror, "I'm not ready for this." He hung his head.

Izabella laid a hand on his shoulder and squeezed. "Your father wasn't ready either. Don't worry. Everything will work out. You are now a husband and a father of twin sons; it is time to continue your destiny and become King. I am looking forward to downgrading to Queen Mother."

"Truly?"

She nodded her head, "No responsibilities, no daily duties. I can spend all my time with your father and your sons. It is what I want most right now."

"That is what I want for you as well. Okay." He stood and brushed his pants to remove any new wrinkles. "I'm ready."

Izabella smiled and escorted her son to the Throne Room.

⇐ ⇒

The Throne Room was brightly lit and richly decorated. When William and Izabella approached the Head Stewart, he rang a bell in his hand and called out loudly, "Crown Prince William and Queen Izabella."

All eyes turned to them, and a hush fell over the crowd.

William and his mother walked through the center of the crowd up to the throne platform. Princess Emily stood off to one side with two handmaidens, each holding an infant. She approached her husband and curtsied. He kissed her hand, pulled her to her feet, and brought her around to stand next to him. Queen Izabella kissed William on the cheek and then went to find her seat.

Standing in front of the King's Throne was the King's bishop. William walked up the steps and knelt in front of the elderly man.

The bishop welcomed everyone to the coronation of Crown Prince William. He explained what was expected of a King.

"Please rise." The bishop said at last. William rose and turned to the audience. "I present to you King William, the first of his name. His wife, Queen Emily." He held his hand out to her as she approached, "and Princes Robert and Wesley."

The room erupted in cheers.

The side doors opened with a flourish, and servants rushed in carrying large trays loaded with meat, cheese, fruits, and vegetables.

The new King and Queen filtered through the crowd, greeting all their guests.

As the evening waned, the women started to disperse and retire to their rooms. Queen Emily was the last woman to retire. She kissed King William quickly on the cheek before departing.

After the door to the Throne Room closed behind her, a large, imposing-looking man walked up to the new King. "Now that the women have left us, let us find some spirits and speak more freely," He boomed in a thick accent.

"By all means, this way," King William said, gesturing to a door behind the thrones. The three other kings in attendance joined them, leaving the dukes and lesser lords to their conversations.

King William led the kings into the king's private study. He shook his head, *My private study*, he thought to himself grimly.

"Welcome to the elite class, young man," the same King said, slurring slightly. A petite maid curtsied as he took a glass off her serving tray. He eyed her and slapped her bottom as she walked by. She jumped with a squeak of surprise, nearly dropping the rest of the drinks. The King barked out a loud, harsh laugh. "You and your father have too light a hand with your servants," he said far too loudly.

"I will keep that in mind, King Roogan."

"Oh, please, titles are for show. Call me Victor." He slapped William on the shoulder. "So, William, my boy. As the newest to our elite class, do you have any questions on how to control your populace?"

"My father has instructed me on how to govern my citizens," William replied.

"Govern! Pah! You are just like your father. You manage your flocks and herds, you govern your counsels, you *control your citizens*," he emphasized. "If you rule with a loose fist, you will have nothing but trouble."

"My father had a different philosophy, with all due respect."

He waved his hand dismissively. "Your father treated his kingdom as one large mews. People are nothing like birds, boy."

"William, if you don't mind. I have heard rumors of your ruling fist Victor. How many uprisings and revolts have you had in the past year?" Another King asked.

Victor glared at him before answering, "Only three this year. You have to rule with an iron fist. This business of treating your people like a falcon is, pardon the pun - for the birds," he said with a slight growl.

William looked at Victor for a moment. "I don't know. My people are well-fed, and we ensure that trade routes are open and safe. My people can obtain all they need. We have very little poverty as long as they are willing to work and follow the law. Work well, remain obedient, and you are rewarded. Keep them looking at the hand that feeds them, and they remain loyal."

"Pash," Victor snarled. "Keep them wanting more, always looking for more… that is the way to rule. If they fear you, they will stay in line."

"You have had three uprisings just this year. They don't sound like they fear you," the other king said, astonished.

"It is a balance, I admit. Fear and reward are used equally. Last year, there were six or seven uprisings. I cut down on the public executions. I showed them that I could be merciful. Only those involved in the uprisings are punished now."

"You used to punish those not involved!" The same king exclaimed.

"To whom am I speaking to?" Victor said, rounding on the other man.

"I am Consul Theodor Parrish," he said with a bow.

"Consul? Not a King?"

"I was elected by the people to govern them."

"Election! You are not worthy to be in our presence."

"I invited him," William said with a scowl.

Victor nodded his head and then turned back to the Counselor.

"Tell me, Theodor, how does this election process work?" Victor sneered.

"The people select people they trust to rule over them. Most decisions are made by vote. Everyone has a voice in the process."

"That is a strange way to rule, but I have heard nothing but good things from your Kingdom," William said.

"While I do not agree with your methods, I must admit it is better than Victor's."

"You dare insult me while I am standing before you!" Victor roared.

"Please, gentleman. We are equals here and can remain civil despite our differences. We each rule our people in our own way. Let us agree to disagree and remain peaceful," William said, coming to stand between the two men.

The other two kings remained quiet, only nodding in response.

"Fine, but your way of rule will not last. As I said, only an iron fist and complete control will last. People are stupid, nothing but sheeple most of them are. Treating them with respect only due to the noble birds we hunt with, or letting them govern themselves is failed for doom and destruction. You will see - one day. Your rule can not last; only the strong can rule. I have had enough of weak men. I will be leaving in the morning." He tossed his glass into the leaping flames of the hearth. It shattered against the stones, the contents hissing in the fire, and stormed out of the king's study, slamming the door behind him.

"My apologies, William," Theodor said with his eyes downcast. "I did not mean to ruin the evening."

William waved his concerns away, "That man has never gotten along with anyone."

"And I did not mean to offend your way of rule. It is just a strange concept to me. If you treat your population like a bird, you only give them just enough to survive and nothing more to keep their loyalty."

"But they are cared for, content, and fed. What more could they hope for?"

"True freedom. Freedom to succeed."

"But with the freedom to succeed, they have the very real possibility to fail," William said cautiously.

Theodor pondered his words for a moment, "That is true, but I would rather have the chance to succeed with the possibility of failure in the back of my mind than live in complete fear of my ruler or even under the passive one that thinks they know what is best for me. Freedom to try, to choose their path, to truly create unfettered. That is the only way a country can truly grow and become prosperous. With only the sky as the limit to someone's potential, it is truly amazing what people are capable of."

It was now King William's turn to ponder his counterparts' words. "I hear your viewpoint, but for my people, I need to govern them the way it has always been done. To change now would ruin their lives. My people are simple people with simple needs. We supply them with all they need. Putting the stress of possible failure on them would be a fate worse than death. Their King knows what is best for them, and I will be the best King yet. As my father told me - to train a falcon… to govern a people."

"Your rule might just turn out to be the worst one yet, with all due respect. Victor's people could very well overthrow him because of his cruelty. Your people, however, will be too complacent to see the veiled mistreatment. People are not animals, while your birds are well treated as animals go, it is no life for a person. No life at all."

King William stared at the Consul with a shocked expression. No one questioned a King's judgment. No one dared.

"I bid you all a goodnight." King William departed, leaving the three men behind. A hard scowl on his face, questions buzzing in his head, and doubt creeping into his heart.

This way, my father's way, was the right way to govern people. It has to be. It was the way it always was. The people loved my father. They will love me, too. I must care for the people, hold their hands, and protect them from themselves, King William thought to himself.

Consul Parrish watched him go, shaking his head. "Kings and tyrants would never learn there was a better way," he whispered, the words trailing after William unheard.

Thank you for reading my allegorical novella. I hope you were able to decipher the message.

Fantasicalrealmpublishing@gmail.com
www.FantasticalRealm.com